A
Season
to Be Born

A
Season
to Be Born

SUZANNE ARMS

Photographs by John Arms

HARPER COLOPHON BOOKS
Harper & Row, Publishers
New York, Hagerstown, San Francisco, London

Photo credits:
Shannon Dunn, p. 4 top
Susan Snyder, p. 4 bottom
Suzanne Arms, pp. 6, 27 bottom, 31 bottom,
46, 104, 105
Jan Schnur, pp. 45, 56 bottom, 63 bottom, 65
Gino August Sky, p. 63 top
Edward Boyce, M.D., pp. 79, 80, 81
Back cover photograph: Suzanne Arms

The lines on p. 50 are taken from "On Children" reprinted from *The Prophet* by Kahlil
Gibran, with permission of the publisher, Al-
fred A. Knopf, Inc. Copyright 1923 by Kahlil
Gibran; renewal copyright 1951 by Administra-
tors C.T.A. of Kahlil Gibran estate, and Mary
G. Gibran.

A SEASON TO BE BORN

FIRST EDITION: HARPER COLOPHON
BOOKS 1973

LIBRARY OF CONGRESS CATALOG
NUMBER: 72–12247

STANDARD BOOK NUMBER: 06-090323-6

76 77 78 79 80   12 11 10 9 8 7 6 5

To Molly

A
Season
to Be Born

Is having a baby what I've really wanted all these years and denied my-self?

I've always been around children. Other people's children. First, as a babysitter. Then as a nursery school teacher. And again when I had my dance class by the sea.

There are times of course when I can't stand being around any kids at all. But I always get back to them somehow. And every time I do, I find one or two that really move me. I want to say, "Come, live with me. Be mine." I can never forget those lovely children.

John and I moved into a cottage on the beach a few years ago. We couldn't resist the water, the air, the sea gulls, the space.

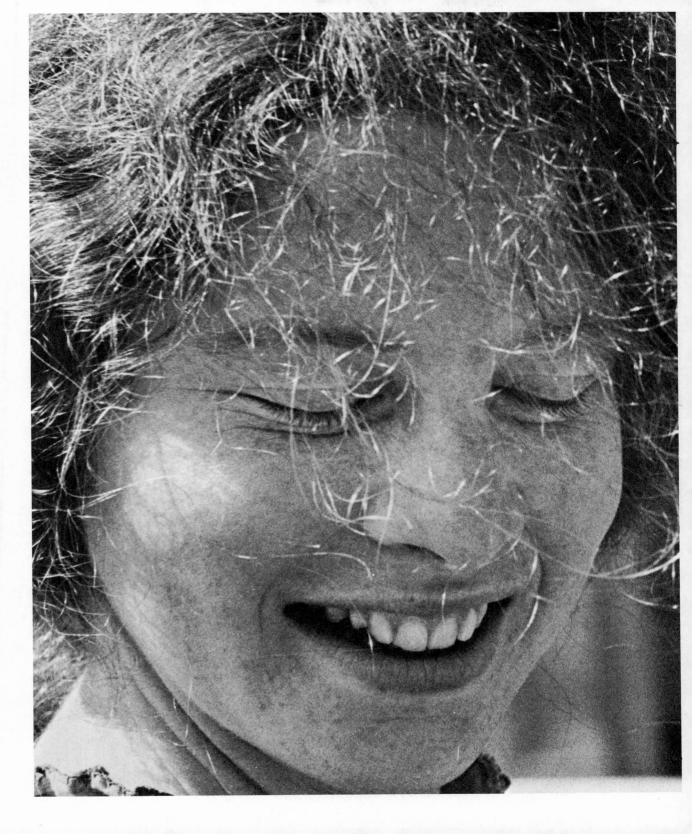

I didn't realize that allowing a baby to grow in me would take a leap of faith and daring. Planning my life, trying to prepare for everything, got me just so far. Then I had to simply close my eyes and go. Leap I did, and happily. I gave up taking birth control pills, and we eagerly awaited a missed period. Then came a day when we felt we knew the exact moment the baby was conceived: I think we were right.

My last period ended November 27th, I think, or on whatever day Thanksgiving was. That day we had dinner with friends who live hours south of us. We were temporarily without a car, so we hitched all the way home carrying the half-eaten turkey in a huge plastic bag. It was easy getting rides. People were curious about us with that bag.

My head is full of thoughts, and I am
full of questions.

Finally I couldn't put off a talk with a doctor any more. I made an appointment with Dr. Miller. When I arrived at his office one Thursday morning, everyone of the fourteen chairs was taken by a pregnant woman who seemed at least eight and one half months along. Several more large-bellied women were standing around the room. They all looked at me with my flat stomach as if I were in the wrong place.

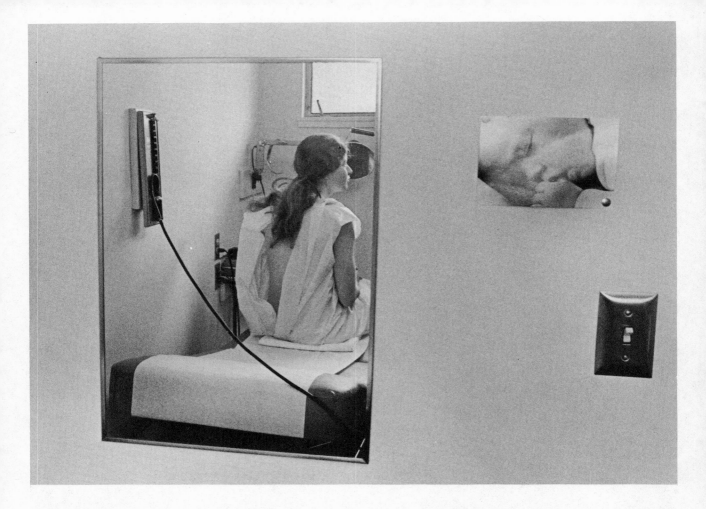

Dr. Miller shares his practice with several other doctors. I met them all— Dr. Miller, Dr. Moss, Dr. Boyce, Dr. Winch. I'm in good hands. During the pregnancy, I'll get to know all of them well. Then when the baby arrives, whichever doctor is on duty will handle the delivery. I guess this will be okay.

Two of the doctors checked me all over during my first visit and confirmed John's and my suspicions. The baby was probably conceived on the day we had thought. That's lovely.

Nausea! There's nothing worse. Why can't I just throw up when I feel sick? What did that old philosopher say? "I am nauseous, therefore I am?" No, that's not right, but it fits! I must be alive, I feel so sick.

The only way I can get relief from nausea is by going to sleep, and I'm really getting good at that. I've been slumbering peacefully through most of this month. Whenever John and I go in the car, we take a quilt for me to cuddle myself in. I can barely stay awake long enough to see us leave town.

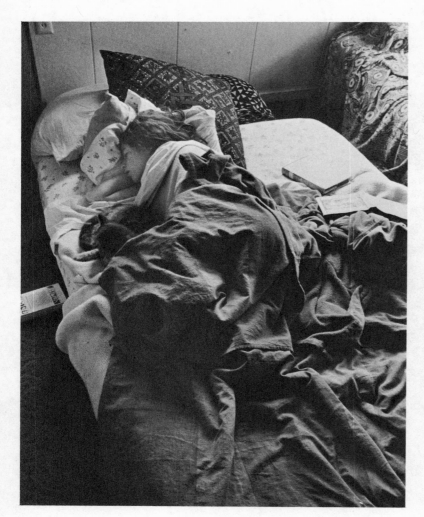

I hear friends knock on the door, very softly as in a dream. John always has to say the same thing: "Suzanne's in bed." It's 10:00 a.m. and Suzanne's in bed. Now 3:00 p.m. and Suzanne's in bed. It could be a visit by the Queen, and Suzanne would be in bed. I don't wanna do anything.

Today I went to my friend Pam's looking for *anything* to settle the creeps. If she told me Elmer's Glue would work, I'd gulp it down. I've been trying lately to drink Golden Seal tea, because the natural foods people swear by it. I wonder why? It makes me feel woozier than ever. Pam fixed a pot of peppermint tea for me. I drank it all, and during the next hour I had complete freedom from nausea. Maybe if I could down a few gallons of peppermint tea every day, I'd be fine.

John brought me a copy of *Let's Get Well* by Adelle Davis to see if she had any ideas for treating nausea. And she does! She says: "vitamin B_6 has been used successfully to stop the vomiting of pregnancy. . . . Pregnant women are commonly deficient in vitamin B_6." Okay, Mrs. Davis, I'm going to give your B_6 a try.

Five days on vitamin B_6 and NO MORE MORNING SICKNESS!

I'm alive! I can eat! I'm gonna buy a
Sara Lee coffeecake and eat it all by
myself!

I got a battered copy of Grantly Dick-Read's *Childbirth without Fear* from the library. Can't put it down until I read the chapter on giving birth in primitive places. The pictures in his book were taken around World War II and show pregnant women in satin panties, bras, garter belts, and long stockings. With white squares pasted over the faces to protect their "identity." My friend Jan and I rolled all over the bed laughing.

I've thought so much about being a
mother but not at all about having a
baby. I can't stand pain. Could I go
through natural childbirth? Every-
body's talking about it. I want to do
it, but it scares me.

I'm beginning to dream about having our baby at home, with John to help, and a midwife assisting. With John close I won't need any drugs.

I feel a movement like a fish swimming in me.

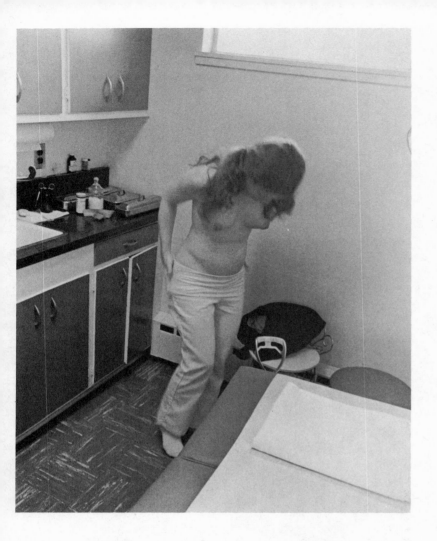

Last night was so lonely. Pitch black outside and wet. I felt so far away from everything warm. John saw me looking melancholy and said, "Suzanne, someday you'll have that little baby of yours. When you do, I believe you'll never be really lonely again." Is it true?

How can I prepare myself for this—an experience different from anything I have ever known? Or is every experience that way—completely different, if we see it for what it is?

I have never felt beautiful but I've always liked my face and filled-out body. I like to look in the mirror when no one is around and scrutinize the person there, make odd faces, and laugh at myself. But looking at pictures of me crying last week really hurt. They're so un-me. Just a pudgy woman. Today I don't feel like that at all. I've tied my hair back, vowed not to wear those baggy farmer jeans till after the baby comes, and put on a dress; I really do feel beautiful. In fact, I feel like I'm a pretty good place for a baby to stay and grow in. Nice, round, firm, with just enough fat all over to make it really soft and safe for the baby.

The sun just came out and lighted the bedroom. Wish I could be happy with just that. Things are strained with John and me this morning.

This afternoon John and I took a walk up the hill overlooking the sea. Sunset is slow in coming this time of year and the days are balmy. We lay down on the dead-end road alongside a meadow and watched swallows zoom over our heads.

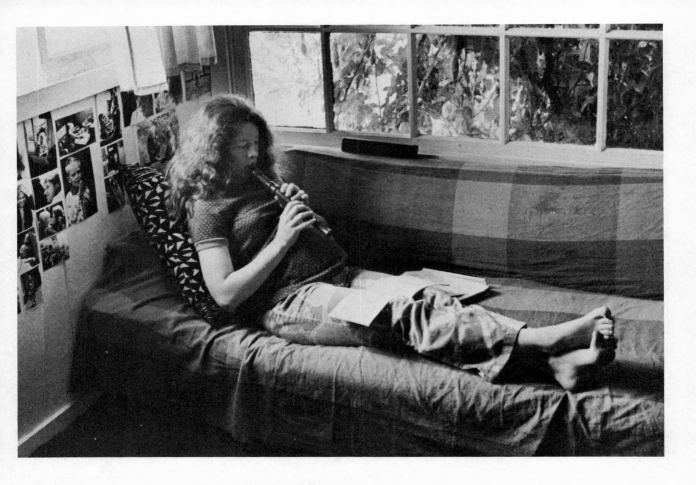

Sometimes I need reminders to take
it easy and not try to be somewhere
I'm not.

I've never loved a dawning so much
as I do today.

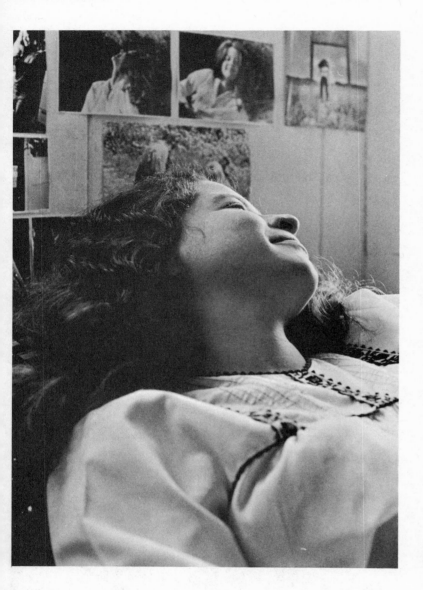

My new blouse feels like a good skin
to face the world in.

Ever since I became pregnant I've been getting more and more pleasure from my sensual feelings. There's some old tightness in me that seems to be losing its hold at last, and I feel all of me expanding.

I ran into a woman from town whom I know only by sight. She stopped me to remark about how fit and pink I was looking and asked how things were going. She told me about her own good times during the last couple of months of pregnancy. I told her about my boundless energy, now that things are really underway, and my desire to clean and cook and sew. She nodded and smiled through the most freckled face I've ever seen on a grown woman. We stood on the street, not knowing each other's name, and felt very close.

At breakfast this morning I completely fell to pieces. Shed a river of tears over the kittens. I thought they were betraying me—after all I'd done for them—by peeing in the bathtub.

I love our home, and the coming home to it. The ride over the mountain. Walking in the door. The cats waiting. Pictures on the wall. The smallness of the cottage. Yet so much room inside.

I rub cocoa butter on my tummy and breasts every morning after showering. The skin has become pink and smooth and I can't help feeling it all the time. The other day we were in the bookstore, and I was absent-mindedly rubbing myself and staring into space. A young woman with a child called to me from across the store, "That's a lovely belly you have there!"

I'm doing something special to each of the baby clothes passed down to me—adding a little embroidery, some ribbon, tiny buttons made from coconut shells. But a baby lies on its tummy a lot; I think I'll embroider the backs of things too.

I am so glad to be called upon to carry someone.

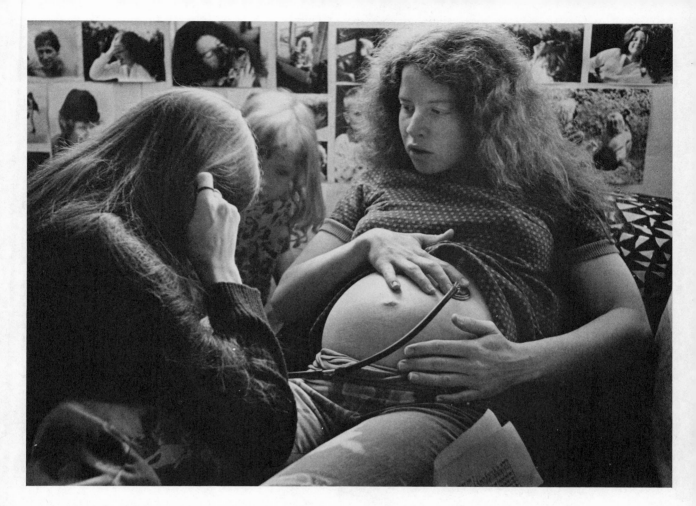

Friends keep coming around now to
pat and thump and poke me. They
want to see. They want to hear. My
sister Linda brought a stethoscope,
and we tried to hear something. No
sounds yet though.

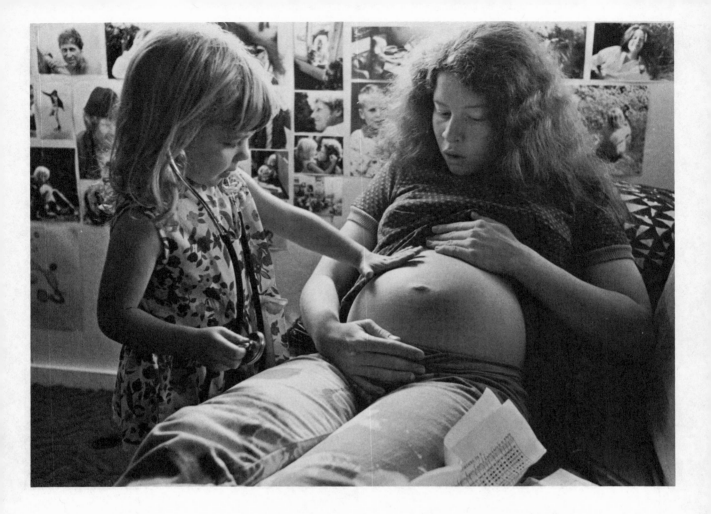

All those years of not feeling any more substantial than a hollow blade of meadow grass.

The only time I remember being in a hospital was several years ago, when I had tonsils removed. I felt then that I was delivering up my body to some absolute power that would fix everything. There was nothing to do but take in the anesthetic and let myself be worked over. The nurses told me afterward that I came out of anesthesia swinging my fists and had to be tied down. I don't remember, but my body must. That time in the hospital I wanted to be passive. Now, the idea of being doped up and worked on as if I were a damaged machine is appalling. I want to do this birth myself. My body must know deep inside how to deliver the baby. Can I get in touch with that knowledge when the time comes?

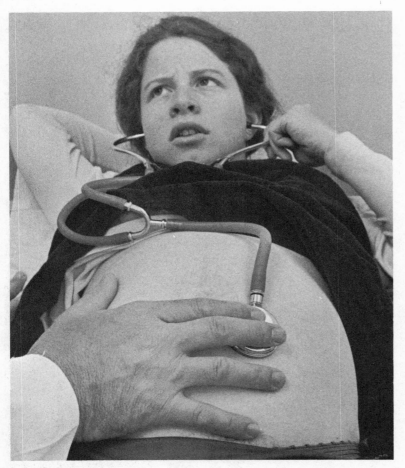

The doctor thinks the baby will come about October 1st. Looks like a Libra. Ever since I saw my weight up to 125, higher than ever in my life, I've begun to feel huge. I remember hearing other pregnant women hassle themselves about getting fat. I never could figure it out. To me they looked beautiful, round and blooming. I assured myself I would never feel that way, and I would love my tummy and all the extra pounds. Well, that's great in theory—but suddenly the day comes when I look in the mirror and my face is round and I really do look like an orange! even holding my stomach in. So yesterday I spent the whole day feeling fat, ugly, and unloveable. Despite every nice thing John has said, I knew he would soon see how unappealing I am. My tummy ached much of the evening, and I woke up with hives on my arms and cheeks.

John's baby dream:

An extraordinarily well-formed baby suddenly appears next to Suzanne while she is lying on the bed. It's a little girl and she has long dark brown hair and lovely round eyes and tight smooth skin. All her features are balanced and well-made.

I keep thinking: I know it will be a lovely girl like this.

45

The kids in the neighborhood come around now and then to check on me and to feel the baby move. On Saturday a couple of mothers dropped off their two-year olds for me to take care of. I took them for a walk down by the creek, we picked some nasturtiums, sucked on honeysuckle, and smelled everything—even the rocks. It didn't seem to bother the kids that rocks don't smell. Or maybe they *do* smell, and children are the only ones who know it. Anyway, we took off our shoes and waded in the creek, found some tiny red leaves to collect and eventually worked our way back home for a warm bath. Little kids are inspiring to follow around. Their attention focuses so quickly on things I haven't noticed. It makes me look with their eyes, and I get as excited as they do. After the bath we went outdoors again and played king of the mountain, the two-year-old's version on a small mound which John had made in the garden.

I do love to feel my tummy. I would
smell it and rub my face in it if I could.

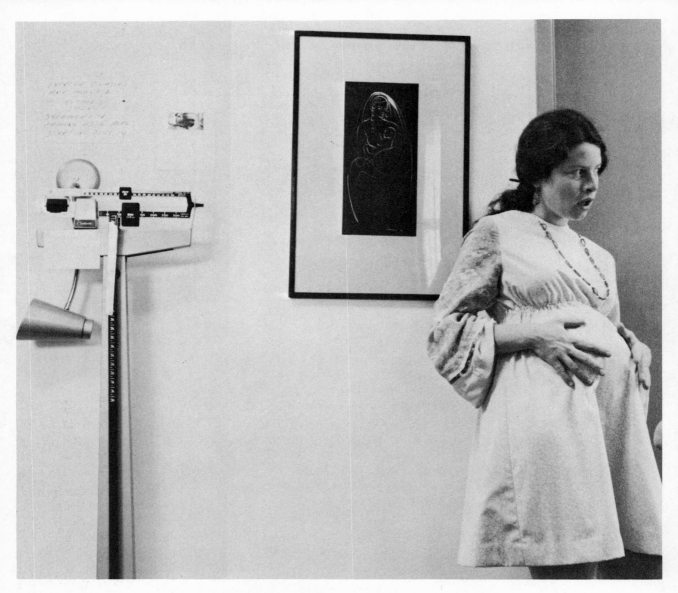

At a friend's house the other night a girl who had her baby ten months ago was saying that her doctor had turned out to be the "dope 'em up, push 'em through" kind. "Next time," she said firmly, "I'm going to find a doctor who believes in the beauty of a woman laboring. No more of this being knocked out for me."

Feeling lumpy today. Lopsided. I always thought pregnant tummies were perfectly spherical. Well sometimes it's just not so.

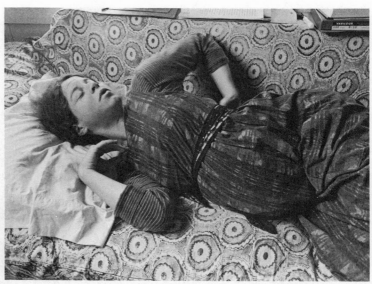

A baby comes into this world from another world. I just know it. If I watch the baby closely, feeling it and responding directly to what it shows me it needs, then I believe I'll do well and grow along with the baby. Gibran's statement has always rung true for me:

Your children are not your children. . . . They come through you but not from you. . . . You may give them your love but not your thoughts. . . . For their souls dwell in the house of tomorrow, which you cannot visit, not even in your dreams.

Yeah. I know that in my heart. What a restful feeling not to feel totally responsible for creating this baby. If I love and nurture it, it wiil grow strong and become what it is meant to become.

My Lamaze exercise class is just too deadly serious. The word "discipline" comes up again and again. Everything is so efficient and hard-nosed. Is this the way it is in the Marine Corps? My teacher is supposed to be helping me learn to relax during labor, and this isn't helping. Guess I'll go back to my dear, gentle yoga teacher.

Our new bed is complete now. John built it high, so that it's level with the window. It's like being aboard a ship. It's too high for a heavyweight like me, and I have to sort of run and leap to get up. *Or,* if John is on the bed, I hold onto him and scramble up. He says he'll make a stool for me to step on, or maybe a ladder.

Making the bed is a gymnastic feat. I bounce around on the mattress, lifting corners to tuck in sheets and pull everything straight. Afterward I flop on the bed and look through the window at the sea and imagine what it would be like to sail away.

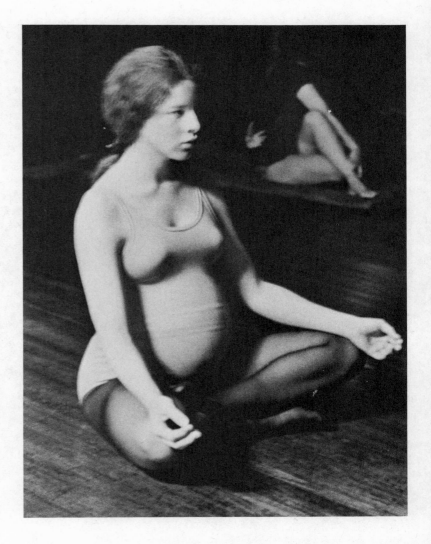

Panting and breathing exercises every day. I'm not very good at correct breathing. It's so hard to do just as they say. I can't manage any more than fifteen or twenty seconds of the panting part. I'll have to learn to do better than this. It's so important for relieving pangs and tension during labor.

Just now closed my eyes and got in
touch with a bad feeling that I've been
having. I'm taking up too much space.
I'm beginning to crowd people.

The sun has just gone down, and I dread the dark evening ahead. Last night's encounter group was too much for me. Why am I having a baby now? I'm just not ready. I've seen a lot of suffering involved with raising kids, a lot of hurting. And I'm so afraid I'll contribute to it. Afraid I too will be hurt.

Is my life as an individual coming to an end? I don't know myself yet. I'm so frightened. Only three months to prepare for everything. Am I going to be able to love my child? Can I deal with the responsibility? I just don't know. I can't possibly do all the growing I have to do in three months. Yesterday I felt so sure. Today all the sureness is gone. What happened to it? Did I ever really have any faith in myself? It seems to have vanished. God, I want to grow! What's holding me back?

And my mother said again today, "Well, let's just hope for a healthy baby."

What is she talking about? Doesn't *she* have any faith? Why wouldn't it be healthy?

We finished a full day's good work early and set off for the Museum of Art. We saw an exhibition of a French photographer's work that charged us up and off we went to a Chinese dinner, jabbering at each other all the way. The baby's been quiet for several days. After dinner in the car I felt a hard lump just beside my navel. Felt like a knee, or a large foot. Nice to know it's still there. I really enjoyed dinner and must have filled every available inch of space surrounding the baby. John and I were wondering whether the baby would feel too much pressure when John lies on me in bed. But the doctor reassured us: "You can't compress a liquid. Don't worry."

I had a fine dance class today and really worked hard on using the abdominal muscles. The baby rested the whole time while I worked. I hope during labor that I'll be able to do the resting and let my body work. I'm sure it knows how.

John and I took one of our early morning beach walks today. The sky was low and bleak. Some white fishing boats were out on the dark water. As we stepped along we began dreaming aloud about living on the Irish Coast someday. John got so excited, he suddenly ran ahead several yards, then turned to watch me as I caught up. I was all bundled in a wooly Irish sweater and a long scarf. John smiled at me and shouted, "Aye, and if you aren't the likes of an Irish Coast woman already!" The instant he said this, a name shot to mind: Molly. I said it aloud. "Yes!" John said. "That's it! The baby's name *is* Molly." And I knew he was right.

Sometimes, waiting is pleasure. Knowing it will happen in good time.

The beach last night was almost totally deserted. The rolling, blowing foam is back, a sign that winter is near. I ran along the water's edge, hoping it might help to get things started inside me. Lying awake early this morning, I listened to the sea and watched the fading stars. What will it be like? How much longer will I have to wait?

I woke up in the middle of the night two nights ago aching and nauseous and thought I must be starting labor. What a strange and frightening way to begin—feeling sick. I thought perhaps my system was cleansing itself and woke John to keep me company. The nausea went on and on so John got up, made tea, and played all of the soothing records we have. He rubbed my back. We talked and it all helped. In the morning John came down with the flu.

I wonder. How could I go through labor if I were sick? Does it ever happen? When I called the doctor this morning for sympathy and to hear his voice, I asked him if women sometimes go into labor very sick. His answer was no. Surprisingly enough, it seldom happens. Come to think of it, I don't know why it should be so surprising. I have so much evidence from my own experience that nature favors a woman who's going to give birth.

A very full feeling today. I'm thick and stuffed like a bulging cabbage.

A Dream:

I have been called into my doctor's office. It's a sterile white room. Sitting at a small business desk is an old employer of mine that I was afraid of and couldn't bear. She looks up from reading my chart and says, "Well, Suzanne Arms. It says here that you have gained 26 pounds. That is disgusting!"

I feel like a little kid. "Yeah, I know, Miss Allbright. But I just love to eat. And I've been feeling so good. Guess I just thought I'd let things happen naturally. You know?"

"Hmm. Well, you're going to be very sorry, Suzanne. You are ruining your spleen. It's no wonder that you're breaking out all over your chest. It's repulsive, the way you eat."

I wake up, guilty as hell, and lie in bed for twenty-five minutes wondering if I should skip breakfast.

I'm depressed. It's getting harder and harder to get close to a plate of food.

The food cravings I've had aren't quite what other pregnant women have told me about. Odd combinations like milkshakes and mashed potatoes, or crackerjack and coke don't interest me. What I long for are certain things I ate when I was six or seven years old. Foods which always made me feel cozy like shredded wheat with warm milk, or egg noodles with butter which I used to fix myself as a snack on Sunday evenings. At home we always ate Sunday dinner at midafternoon. By dark, though, I would go rummaging

around trying to fill the Sunday night emptiness that I felt during those years. These Sunday blues have largely passed now, but shredded wheat with warm milk—the way my brother taught me to fix it—still helps me through insecure times.

I think I'm getting myself together now. Can I hang on to this serenity in a cold hospital?

I never thought it would come to this. I can't reach over my stomach to get to my feet. John has to lace up my hiking boots!

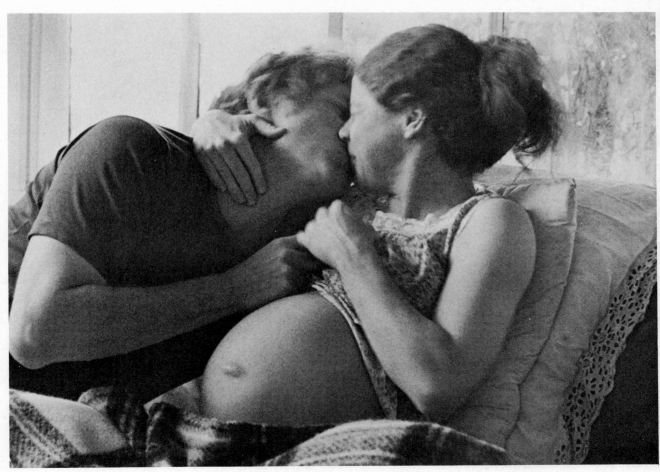

It's hard to imagine. I've walked steep trails, scrubbed floors, danced long hours until my bones ached, but trying to imagine what a day of laboring for a baby might be is beyond me. I'm looking forward to it, but I'm frightened too. Wish I could be cool about it. After all, it'll just be one day in my life—one special twenty-four hours when I know everything in my body will be working for me.

I really do look like an orange!

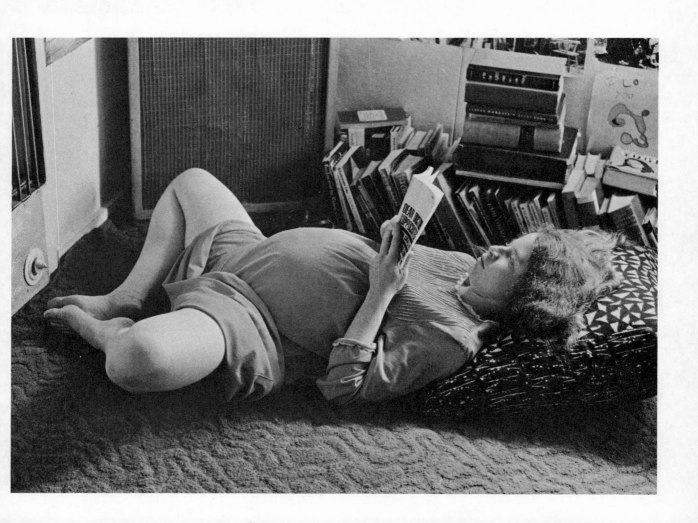

Every morning now I find myself waking up and turning excitedly to look at the empty baby basket that waits on top of our bureau. I feel like a child counting the days until Christmas.

Sometimes it seems as though I've been pregnant all my life. I can't remember being unpregnant.

I can see things about myself these days that surprise me. Yesterday, I went to see my younger sister, after hearing from a neighbor she was in trouble. I left the car and headed toward Linda's door like some commanding all-powerful mother. John mentioned later how my whole bearing had changed. Have you ever suddenly awakened to see yourself as others see you? It's startling. For some time after John's comment, I felt exposed and silly. I know that I have neither the right nor the wisdom to tell Linda how to live. I just hope that I'll still be able to see this when I'm a real mother, and my child is Linda's age. Deep inside, I think Linda knows best how to live. She doesn't need my sermons.

close. My friend Sunny said her two easiest labors came after doing a ton of physical work around her house on the day of birth.

I've been getting a case of the "tidies" —the urge to clean, sort, arrange, paint, throw out, and just *do.* Friends tell me this happens when the time is

I've gradually filled my hospital suitcase. And I mean I've *filled* it! John can barely zip it closed for me. At first I was just going to lay in a few necessities. Then I started adding things, and now it looks like I'm going on a long holiday.

There's a bedside candle. A Japanese novel. A picture of sand dunes and distant white caps to pin to the labor room wall. A copy of Alan Watt's *Wisdom of Insecurity*. A chart I drew with felt-tipped pens that shows how labor progresses. Some lovely nature cards to mail to friends when the baby

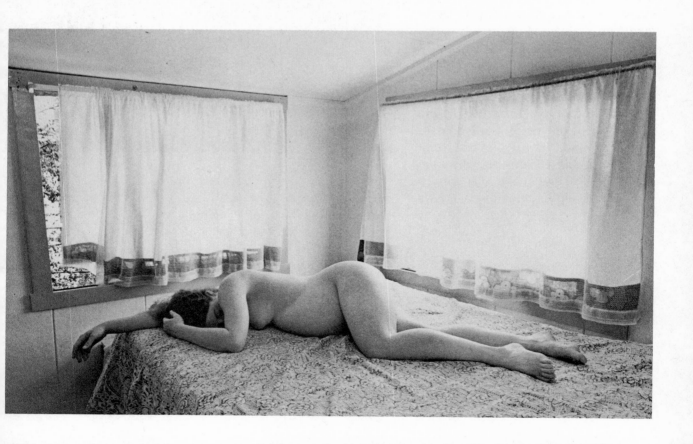

comes. If I haven't been carried to the hospital by tomorrow, I think I'll empty everything out of the bag and start over. I'll try to be sensible about it this time. The only reason I want all that baggage anyway is to give me a sense of security. But it's no use. I'm going for a ride over the falls, and I'll be too busy keeping my head above water to worry about clutching all my belongings as I go.

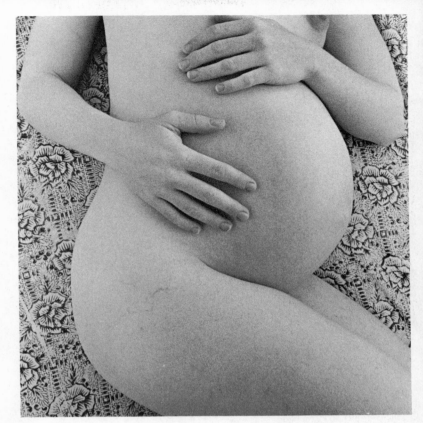

Things aren't really ready. I want to be alone. Don't want to chitchat. Everyone's asking, "When is it going to come?" Too many people with anxious faces. TOO MANY QUESTIONS!

It's nice feeling knowing that this baby is one thing in my life that I can't force or organize or schedule. I just have to let it happen. The baby isn't going to be born till it's ready. I'd like my whole life to be like that. John and I have long ago given up scheduling our days and making lists, but sometimes the lists write themselves in my head. Does the baby feel all of my anxieties through the umbilical cord?

Dr. Winch examined me and said that the cervix is 50 to 80 percent thinned out today. He was able to put the tip of his finger through the cervix and feel the membrane which surrounds our baby.

Well here it is!

I woke suddenly half an hour ago feeling a flooding surge of water and leaped out of bed just in time to save the sheets. Save the sheets from what, I'm not sure. Since childhood, I remember hearing women talk about water breaking, and I always asked myself how would I dry the mattress if it happened to me in bed. I promised myself not to wet the sheets, and by God I didn't. Dear God, why am I worrying about bed sheets now? I'm having a baby!

John isn't here. He's walking on the beach. John, please come back! Can you hear me! I'll try to stay quiet now. I'll start a warm bath and get in carefully—and just wait.

It can't possibly be time yet! I'm just a kid! I can only pant for twenty-six seconds. I'm simply not ready. The baby is easier for me to carry around now. I wonder if I could go for ten months instead of nine.

John's home. As usual, he's got everything under control. He called the doctor, and the two of them conferred about me with utter calm. Men!

They've decided to wait until the contractions start before John packs me into our VW bus for the trip to the hospital.

John's putting towels under me and

covering me all over with our best blankets.

My body's made of rubber.

I've been so excited waiting for labor to begin, and now that it's started, I can't sit down, I can't rest, I can't do anything I'm supposed to do. Brenda just ran up the hill to be with me. We've decided that it might help to bathe and eat. Okay, that's what I'll do.

John's running around the cottage with his own case of the tidies. I love him.

Brenda's fixing a plate of filet of sole and green beans. It may sound funny at a time like this, but I'm ready to eat every bit of it. Please bring it, Brenda.

My body feels unreal.

Five hours after water broke, labor began. That first contraction—it was unmistakable. Nothing I had ever felt prepared me for the sharp, twinging pull inside my vagina. But I knew what it was immediately.

Within an hour, contractions were coming four minutes apart and lasting fifteen seconds. John called the doctor to give him this information, and the doctor told him to get me to the hospital right away. I got out of bed and paced back and forth in front of my closet. What do you wear to have a baby?

I chose my tweed woolen skirt. And my favorite navy sweater to keep

warm in. Knee socks, too. The night was cold and black.

John packed my side of our VW bus with pillows and blankets. He grabbed the suitcase I'd packed and repacked, and we pulled out of town. John honked and honked as we passed Brenda's darkened house, and then Pam's.

We bounced and jiggled the whole fifty minutes over our mountain road and into the city. John held my hand tightly as he drove and kept reminding me to relax, to breathe deeply, to keep the faith. His pocket watch told us the contractions were coming two and one-half to three minutes apart and were lasting about twenty seconds. At this rate, I was sure the baby would come very soon.

We pulled into the vacant parking lot at French Hospital at 1:00 A.M. It was beginning to rain, so we rushed to the door. I shuddered to think what it would be like to have my first baby in the cold rain.

Most of the lights were out in the hospital. Only the lobby looked alive. I went in and walked proudly toward the lady at the switchboard. "I'M SUZANNE ARMS, AND I'M GOING TO HAVE THIS BABY!" There couldn't be any doubt, since at that moment I grabbed a nearby chair and sank into it to have another contraction. In an instant a wheelchair appeared through an elevator door—for me. John helped me into it, and I was wheeled into the elevator and taken down two floors to the basement. I smiled at everyone along the way, but tears kept spilling on my navy sweater.

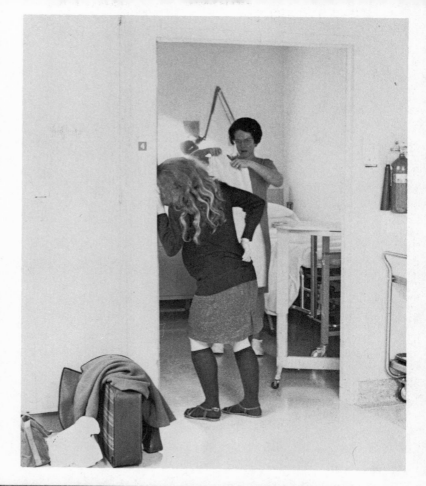

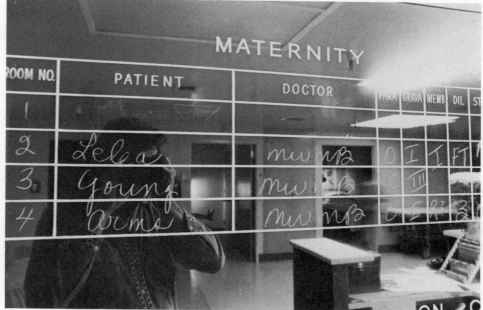

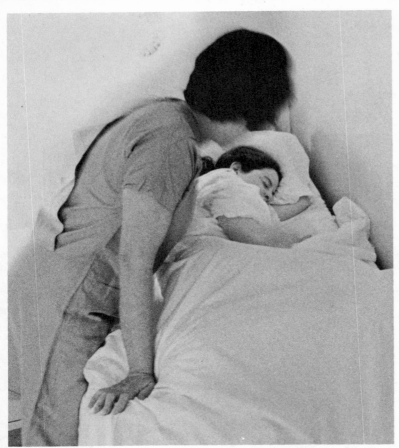

The middle of night and I'm wheeled into a dinky basement room in this immense hospital. I'm so grateful for my husband's presence. It's the way it should always be—the father and mother together for the birth of their baby.

A tall, serious nurse has told me to get undressed and into a waiting gown. "How am I doing?" I wonder.

"You're tense," she says. "See? Your palms are clammy. You'd better lie back and relax. Close your eyes and start breathing in the right way, dear. It's going to be a while."

No enema and no shaving here at French Hospital. They've done away with these procedures. Good! But right now it doesn't matter to me either way.

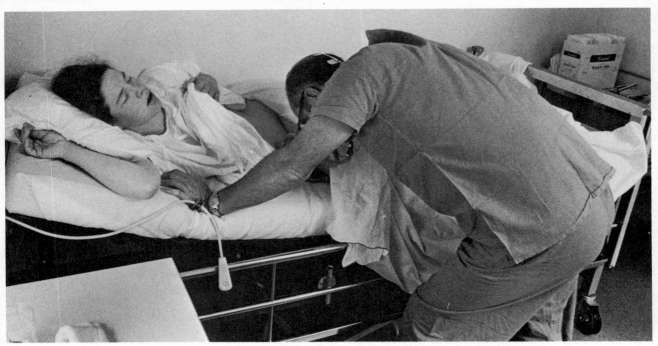

The baby's heartbeat is a high rapid flutter. I have to concentrate to hear it. Sounds as if it comes from a hummingbird.

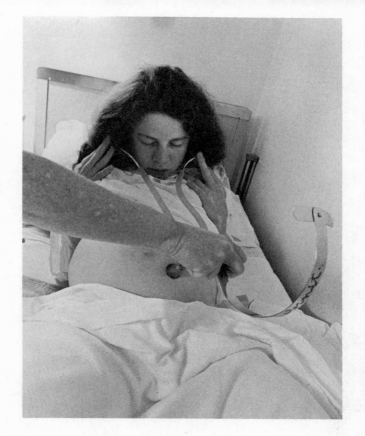

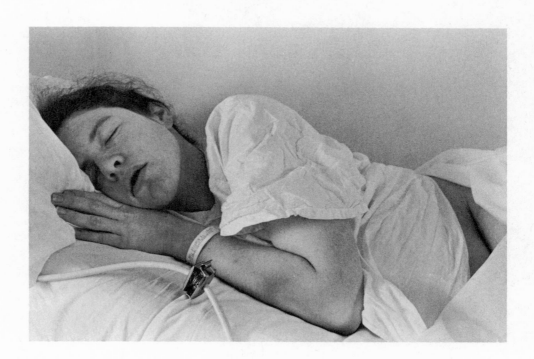

Moments when I lose my breathing rhythm I descend into darkness, and I want somebody's help to climb back up.

Now I know what that cool-headed teacher of the Lamaze class meant when she spoke of staying on top. I thought she meant staying in control. But no. Being loose, accepting, flowing, and trusting that each contraction will pass and bring the birth closer. That's the idea.

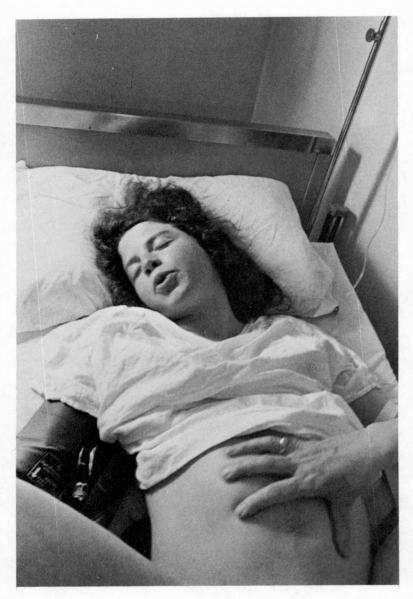

After several hours of labor I've become confused, delirious. But I think I've suddenly found a rhythm I can follow. Way out on the edge of my memory there's this friend's voice telling me that her own contractions were like riding waves. I've seized upon this image, and as each contraction begins I close my eyes and picture myself climbing a wall of ocean water. It feels good. And while I keep this picture in mind, I roll my head from side to side on the pillow and count my breathing. I blow softly and whisper each number . . . one . . . two . . . three. . . . By the time I reach ten (later it'll be twenty, and finally twenty seven), I feel the wrenching inside come to a peak, and it's time to ride the wave down, blowing and counting, riding on my back, outstretched and relaxed under the warm sun.

Wish there were windows in this stark room. Nothing to look at but that monotonous round clock. The hands seem to stand still, then make little leaps forward: 7:00 . . . 7:15 . . . 8:00 . . . 8:05. . . .

Think of the light, Suzanne. Oh, how I wish I could see the sun!

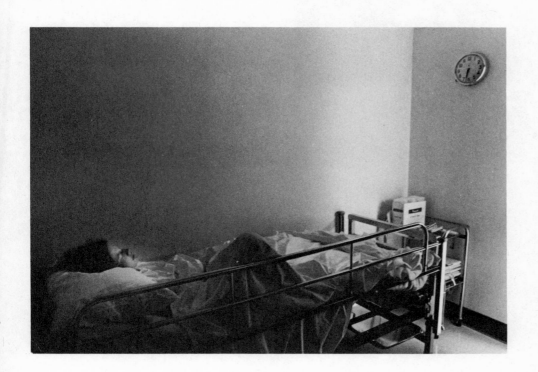

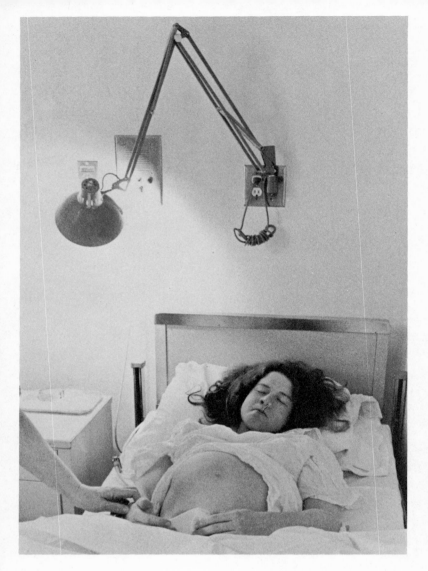

There are hours when I take each hour as it comes and think only of breathing in and out and experiencing the contraction as just another feeling spreading through me. But then I lose my comforting rhythm and begin nervously to count the hours: "Ten o'clock and only six and one-half centimeters dilated. I'm not doing well . . . so tired . . . I want a break . . . just a short break from it all. Please! Then I'll come back and finish.

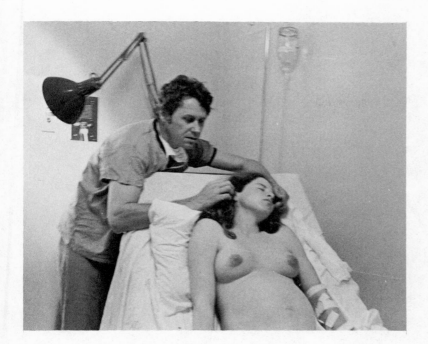

I'll never really know just what it is
like for you, John. Many times I fade
in and out, drift off, dream. When I
return to the labor bed I turn and see
you, still there, quiet and watching.

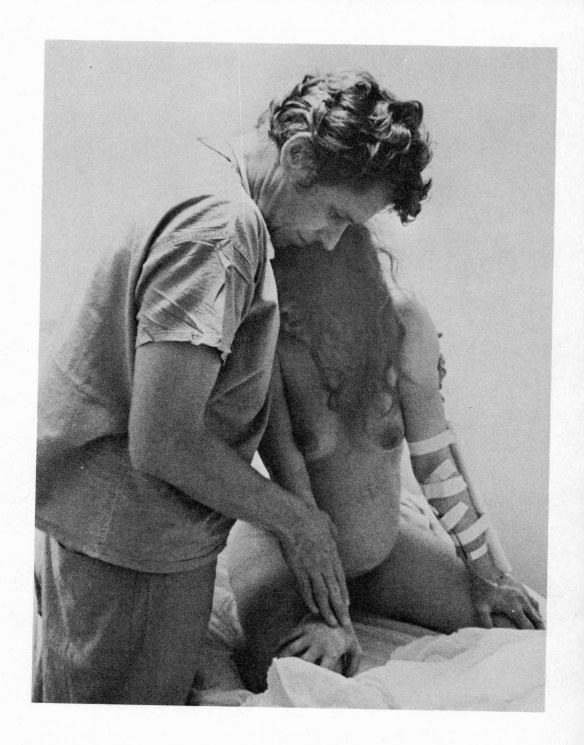

It goes on forever. I wish now I'd done more training to get me through the tired times.

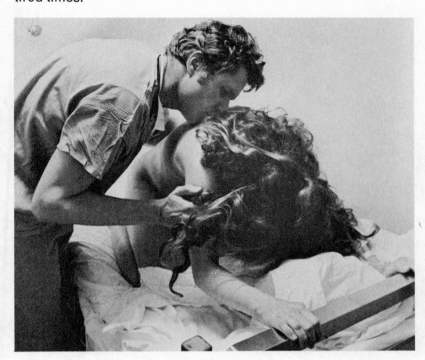

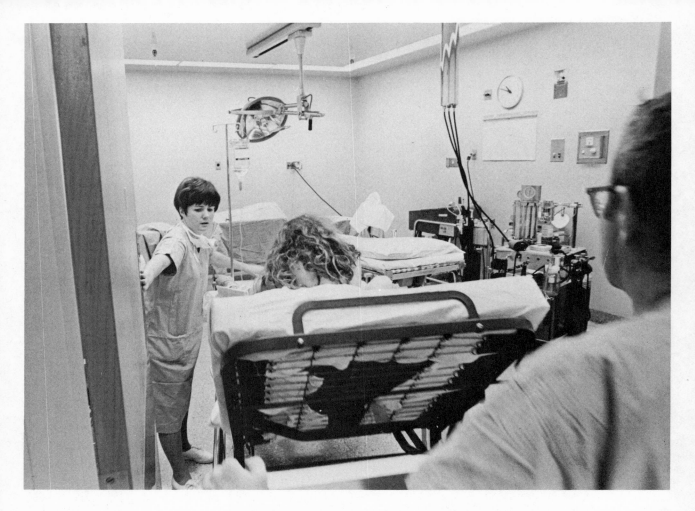

Dr. Boyce is here! And he's going to stay with me now until it's over. I feel I must push. I can't wait! Okay, he says. Go ahead.

All my energy comes from working at relaxing and being passive to doing something at last. I take two deep breaths and then go with the force inside me. It's like the beginning of a tremendously hard race I must win.

Push! HARDER. I couldn't stop pushing now if my life depended on it.

Part of the time I squat Indian style. I've always wanted to have the baby in the same way that women before me have had theirs. So I squat for a while and feel in touch with the past. All women, throughout all time, giving birth.

But my legs burn with fatigue after half an hour. I'm not used to squatting. I'm just not a primitive woman. It makes me sad, but I go back to holding my legs bent and lying propped up against the raised back of the bed.

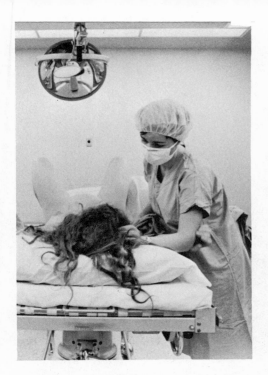

there are more white rooms. Then big doors swing open. We go into a large space, gleaming white and silver. Cold metal all around my hot body. But I don't care. I just want the baby. I wonder if I'll ever have it.

The anesthesiologist is waiting here, and he moves fast. The instant he finds the place with his needle, I feel the pressure inside me slide away. I

I'm getting so tired. If I push much longer, I know I'll just split apart. My spine is like a weak seam.

While Dr. Boyce and John and I decide how to go about things, the pushes keep coming. My body won't stop. But I'm too tired to care what's happening. The white walls move in and out. The room seems to be afloat. The three of us are alone, drifting across an ocean. I don't care anymore. I'll go wherever they take me.

Dr. Boyce opens the door to the outer room and calls to the nurses. People fill my room and lift me up. In a minute I am wheeled naked down a hall on a dolly. I had forgotten there was anything outside my white room. Here

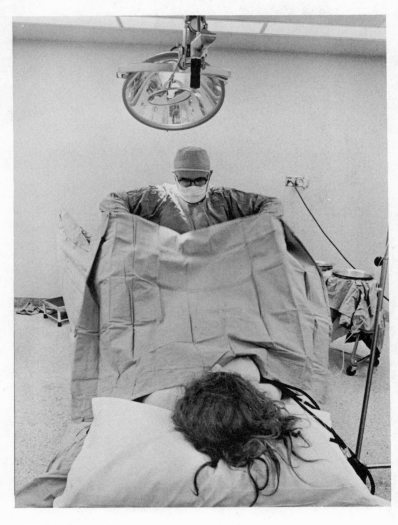

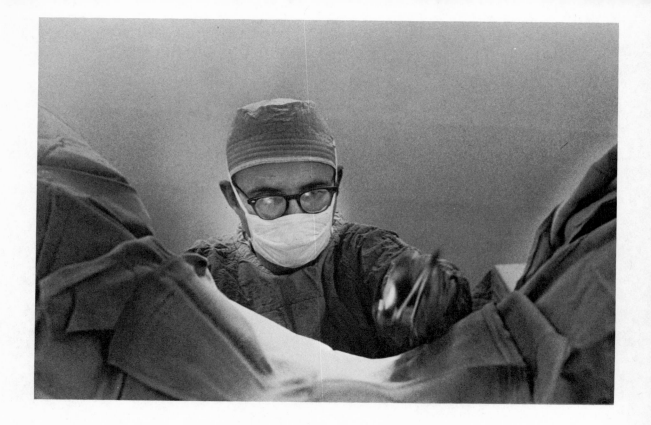

fall back on the table and smile thank you. Thirty hours have passed since my water broke at home. I'm ready to be relieved.

The next twelve minutes Dr. Boyce slowly eases the baby down the birth canal with his spoon-shaped forceps.

And now the moment I've tried nearly all of my life to imagine suddenly comes without me feeling anything! I lie back, and Molly is born.

Even Dr. Boyce is relieved. The baby looks perfect. Everything is blurred, but I sense the smiling faces all around. Thank you, everyone.

When they place her next to me, she is all there is in my life. She's here. And she's fine. She's beautiful. And we're alive. I'd do it again, all over again—yes, I would. To relive this single moment.

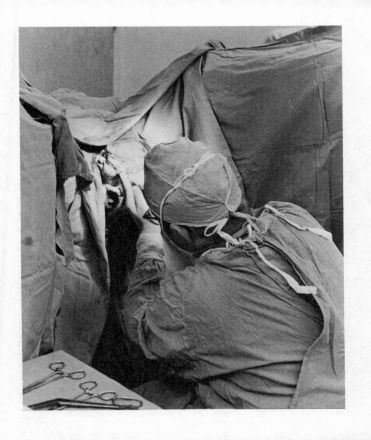

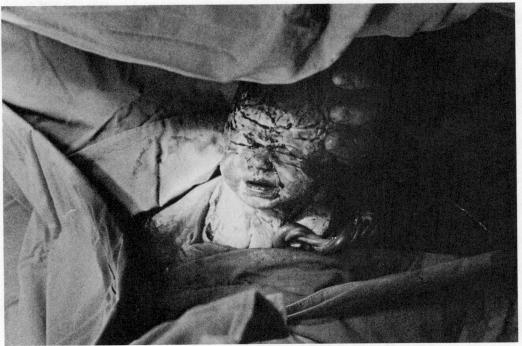

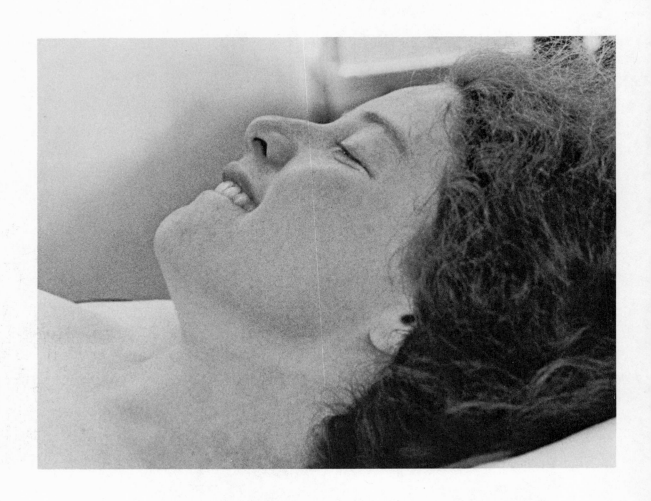

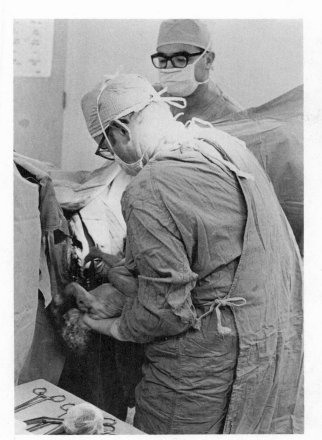
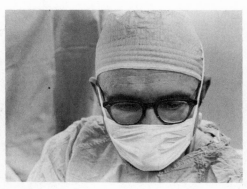
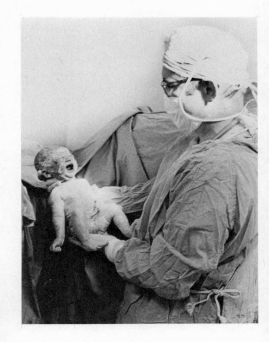
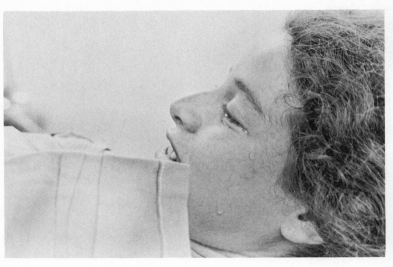
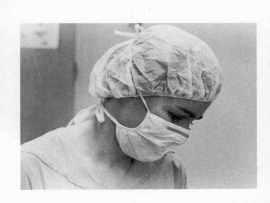

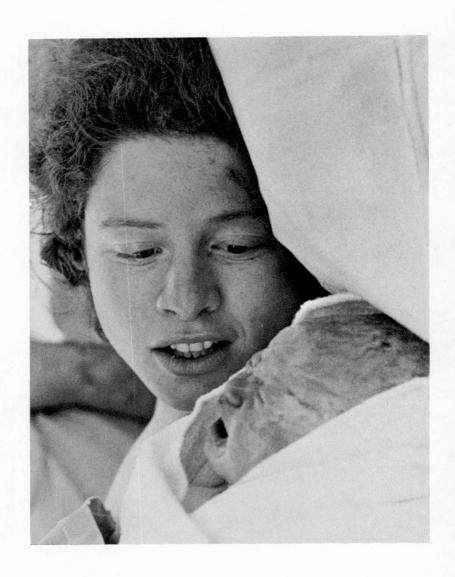

Did she have to be a forceps baby? I wonder if it could have been different if we'd had her at home with a midwife? I guess I'll never know.

Even if I didn't do it all myself, it's okay. Molly's here. She's safe. She made it. I made it.

She had a lot of white creamy vernex on her head, and a thick fluid around those big gray-blue eyes that looked out on everything so calmly.

I remember one moment when I reached so low and was so desperately tired. And then suddenly, I wanted to burst out laughing. A huge joke, some hilarious stage play. For that instant, everything was upside down, but I was riding fine.

Surrealistic impressions: The whole experience like a jig-saw puzzle with pieces missing. All that white. All those walls. Silver instruments and hot lights. Masked faces with warm eyes. People around me urging and inspiring. And the words. You're doing fine, Suzanne. It'll be all right, dear.

After Molly appeared and they brought her around the table to me, I first laughed. I was so relieved. Then I cried so hard that tears ran into my ears and collected in a puddle at the side of my nose. My left arm held Molly, wrapped tight with just her streaked face showing, and my right arm had a lot of gadgetry taped-on for the I.V., so I couldn't move to scratch the tickle. I called to John. He wiped away the puddle of tears and went right to the place that itched as if it were his own.

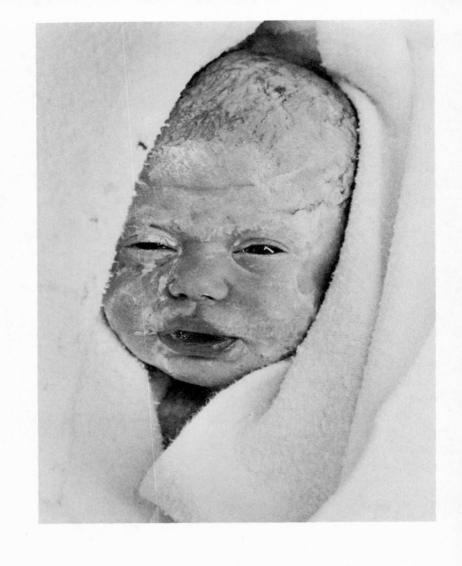

Lying on the dolly in the hall, my body is numb. But I can feel Molly next to me. How long did I lie here saying goodbye to John, with the cool sheets and the bright lights?

Molly was born at 11:29 p.m. What a day, full of nightmarish things. Ending in ecstasy. I'll never forget how the delivery room felt as Dr. Boyce pulled Molly out and John yelled: "It's Molly!"

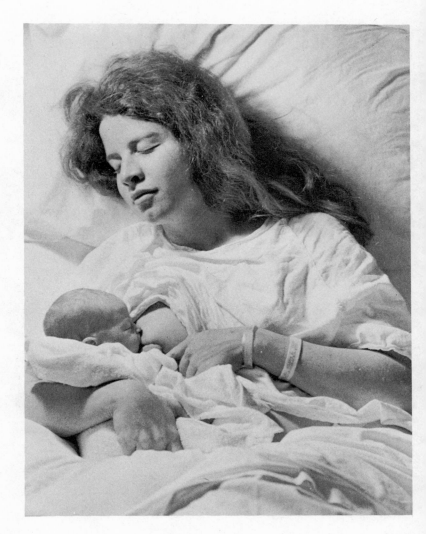

I could nurse the baby, John, Lizzie,
and still take on more. I WANT TO
NURSE!

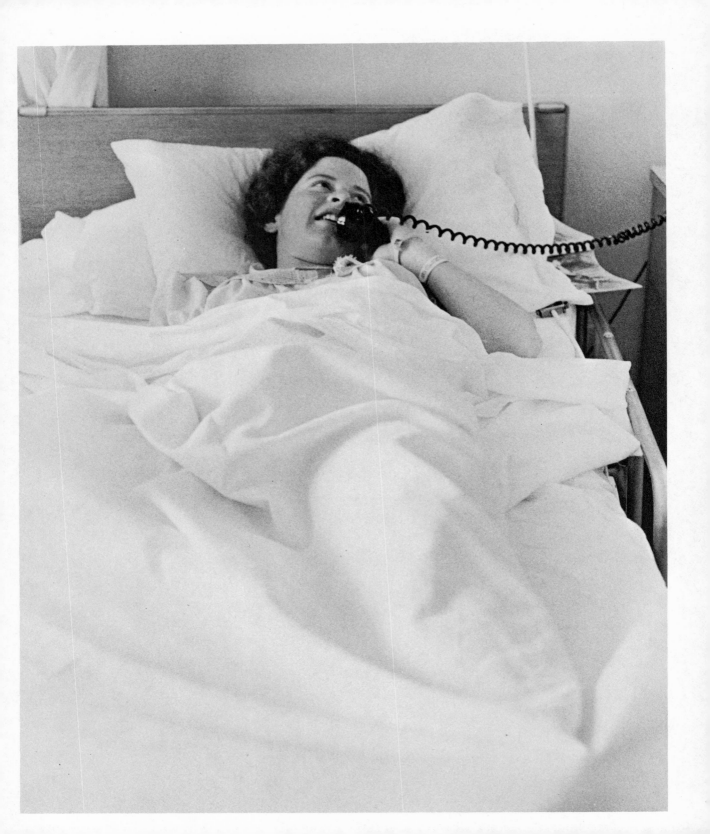

Somebody sent red roses today. I appreciate the thought, but the roses sadden me. They remind me of formal occasions, like strained graduations and funerals. Having Molly has been a wild, almost primitive experience. Nothing formal about it. I love the little yellow flowers that John brought this morning. They're sunny looking like Molly.

Molly's hands. They look transparent in the light. As if she's really not solid yet. She has a way of turning her palms away from her as she sleeps, like a ballerina. John predicted that we would probably see some of these earliest gestures repeated in Molly's later life.

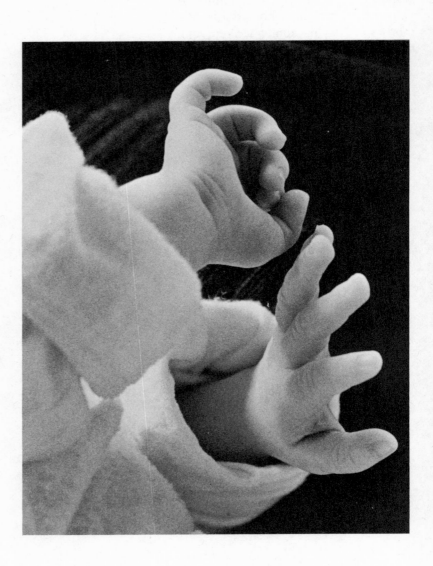

Home. The three of us are home. Molly is a week old today. When people look at her and ask their questions, I feel like the poet who, when asked to comment on his work, could only point to his poem.

When I show the neighbor kids how milk comes out of a breast if I squeeze and press just so, how it squirts from a dozen tiny holes in the nipple, I'm as amazed as they are.

I changed her on the couch today. I watched her draw her body into a fetal position, with knees tucked against her belly and tiny feet crossed and bent flat. How long will she do this—a vision of when she was cuddled up inside of me?

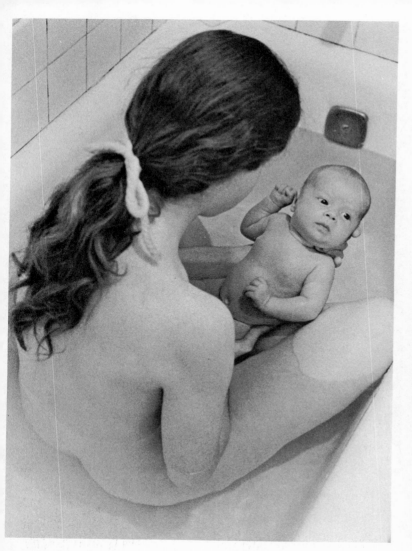

Molly screamed the first time I dipped her in water at the kitchen sink, so John came up with an idea. Why not take off Molly's and my clothes, hold her close to my breast, and while she nurses, slip into the tub with her? I tried it. It works. So that's how we do it now. The water has to be lukewarm for her, not hot the way I like it, but it's worth being a bit chilly to have her content.

At times when she sleeps longer than seems right, I go into the room with my heart pounding to check. God, is she alive? I have to hear her breath and see her little chest move.

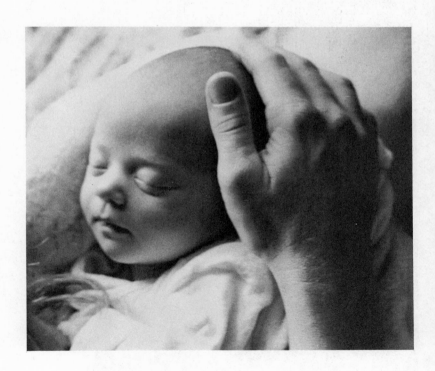

John wants to make love. So soon? I'm worried. Vulnerable. Will I tear open? Can't he understand I'm just not ready?

When I tie the tummy pouch tight and Molly is pressed flat against my chest, I feel invincible. I'll protect you, Molly, always. Until you're grown, I'll keep you safe. *I will.*

Last night, my most frightening night-mare since childhood. Grotesque. Dark. The baby was hurt and I was helpless. I know now what a friend was feeling when he told me that he couldn't possibly survive the death of one of his children.

It's awesome knowing that Molly's very survival depends on me. On my presence to feed and change and protect her. Sometimes in the dead of night I'm jolted out of my sleep by the thought that I might forget all about her. I just can't be an irresponsible kid anymore.

Nursing in public: Yesterday I went to a chamber music concert downtown. I sat in the back of the community center, ready to leave if Molly made a sound. But she was quiet and I nursed her with a light shawl over my shoulder. This morning in the mail I received an anonymous envelope with an Amy Vanderbilt column circled in red. It says women should nurse only in the privacy of the bedroom, or, if out in public, should stay in the car or seek out a restroom. Well, if I followed prudish advice like this I'd spend half my time hiding myself and Molly. They've got to be kidding. I showed the column to Brenda and she was furious. Well, "the times they are a-changin'."

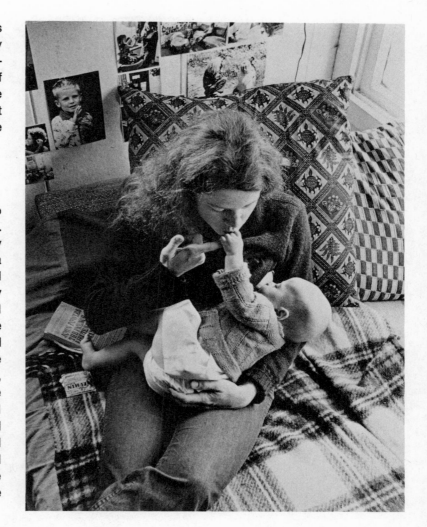

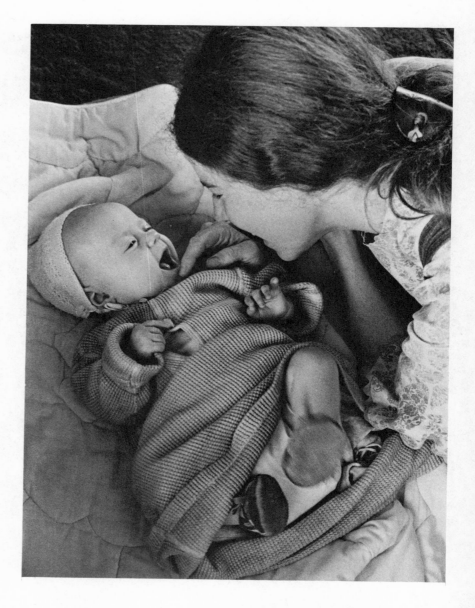

Molly, have you really been here forever? I can't remember there not being a you.

Already, Molly, you're growing and changing so fast I want to catch you and stop you.

You in me. Now, you *and* me.